Meerkat Madness
Flying High

First published in Great Britain by HarperCollins *Children's Books* 2012
HarperCollins *Children's Books* is a division of HarperCollins*Publishers* Ltd,
77-85 Fulham Palace Road, Hammersmith, London W6 8JB

Visit us on the web at
www.harpercollins.co.uk

1

MEERKAT MADNESS FLYING HIGH
Text copyright © Ian Whybrow 2012
Illustrations copyright © Sam Hearn 2012

Ian Whybrow asserts the moral right to be identified as the author of this work.

ISBN 978-0-00-744161-7

Printed and bound in England by
Clays Ltd, St Ives plc

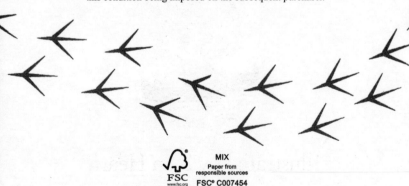

MIX
Paper from
responsible sources
FSC® C007454

FSC is a non-profit international organisation established to promote the
responsible management of the world's forests. Products carrying the FSC
label are independently certified to assure consumers that they come
from forests that are managed to meet the social, economic and
ecological needs of present and future generations.

Find out more about HarperCollins and the environment at
www.harpercollins.co.uk/green

Foreword

The behaviour and adventures of the characters in this book are modelled on those of certain actual meerkats still living in the Kalahari. These creatures wish to remain anonymous to protect their privacy. For this reason, their names and their language have been changed. Any similarity between these characters and any meerkat-stars of stage or screen is purely coincidental.

Furthermore, any resemblance between Oolooks or Whevubins on safari, actual Click-clicks or Sir David Attenborough is purely in the eye of the beholder.

Ian Whybrow

Meerkat Madness
Flying High

IAN WHYBROW

Illustrated by Sam Hearn

HarperCollins *Children's Books*

With love to Amelie, Ella, Fifi and Ted
and with special thanks to Daniela Maimone,
the world famous balloonist and photographer.

Uncle Fearless

sniff

Skeema

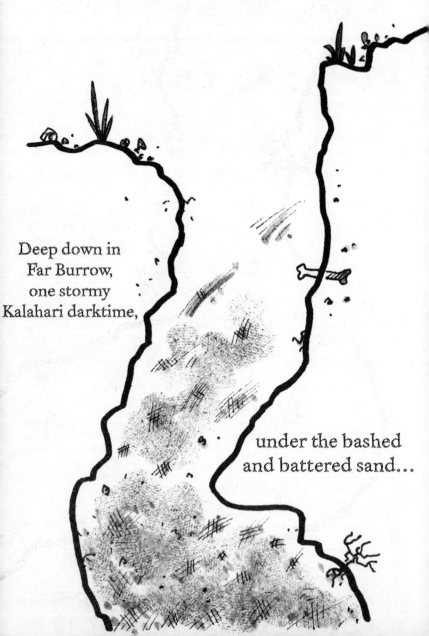

Down...

Deep down in
Far Burrow,
one stormy
Kalahari darktime,

under the bashed
and battered sand...

Here we are.
Curled up calm and feeling
safe in their separate
sleeping chambers,

two snug little bundles of
meerkats were fast asleep.

Little did they know that a creeping enemy was slithering and sliding and feeling its way down the tunnels...

...to swallow them up!

Chapter 1

It was (as you know) a stormy darktime in the Kalahari desert. On the far side of the old kingdom of the Sharpeyes, on the edge of the salt pans, the sky was nasty with fizz-fire and sky-crash.

In one snug chamber the founder members of the Really Mad Mob had rolled together into a ball for warmth. They were the three kits, Skeema, Mimi and Little Dream; and their king and guardian, Uncle Fearless. They were never quite still. The place was jumping with ticks and fleas, so there was a lot of jerking and scratching.

Meanwhile, in another chamber a short distance away, Uncle's new queen, Radiant, lay awake. Normally she slept well. She was not one for worrying and all that nonsense. She was as warm and hearty and cheery as the sun itself and that is why she was called Radiant. She was tucked up tight in the nursery chamber with her four babies. They were a couple of weeks old now, and tiny, clinging, squirming... and the thing was, they were shivering. Their names were Zora the Snorer, Bundle and Quickpaws. Oh, and Trouble.

This is Trouble.

It was the shivering of the babies that woke Radiant up. Soon she became aware that in spite of her own splendid coat of fur, she was cold herself. She couldn't think exactly what the matter was, but she sensed danger. By instinct, she sprang to her paws and sounded the Snake Alert. *Krrrr! Krrrr! Hi!-Hi!-Hi! Krrrooo! Krrrupp!*

Uncle Fearless's sharp ears twitched and in a split second he too sprang to attention. His one eye flew wide open and he jumped up, rousing the kits and sounding the General Alarm – "*Wup-wup! Wup-wup!* Action Stations, everyone!"

"Wha-what is it?" cried Mimi. "What's happening to me, to Mimi?"

"Is it a yellow cobra?" cried Skeema, bristling for a fight. He felt in the darkness for his trusty Snap-snap. To you and me it was a plastic bath-toy crocodile that had been dropped by a small boy on a safari holiday. To Skeema, Snap-snap was the powerful friend and protector he had found on one of his first adventures in the Upworld. He nipped his lime-green tail for luck and made Snap-snap shrill in the darkness. *Skweee!*

"I dreamed I was up in the sk-sky, flying with the b-birds!" stammered Little Dream, his teeth chattering. "Wh-why is it so c-cold?"

None of the worried wakers could see a thing in the total darkness, but Uncle Fearless was straining his ears.

"Silence!" he ordered.

Uncle ran to the heap of sand that served as the main door to the chamber and tested it with his sensitive nose. "Soaking wet and saturated, by all that creeps and crawls!" he shouted. "The rains must have got into the burrow! Stand by, all paws and claws! Make ready to dam the flood!"

None of the kits knew what a flood was, but they knew better than to chatter. They waited for their orders.

"Quick and tricky, now!" urged Uncle. "Batten down the hatches! There's water coming down the main tunnel. We must block off this door!"

With the skill and teamwork that comes with hard practice, the kits dug their long, sharp claws into the damp floor and passed sand and soil through their legs to Uncle.

"Good work, team!" he panted as he piled it into a sizeable dam. "It's holding! That should keep us dry for a moment longer. Now, follow me out through the side-wall. And hurry! There's not a moment to lose!"

The water was trickling into the burrow fast, even down some of the side-passages. As soon as the kits broke out of the chamber, they found themselves in bone-chilling

water almost up to their bellies. The shock of it made Mimi cry out. "*Prrrr!* It's biting me!"

"Keep close and keep moving!" ordered Uncle and he began to call "*Ki-ko! Preeep!*" at intervals. He wanted to let Radiant know that he was safe and not too far away.

"Do hurry, old thing!" came her faint and muffled reply. "The babies are getting awfully chilly!"

"Just as I feared, what-what!" muttered Uncle. "They'll catch their deaths if we don't get them to a warm place, sharpish. Stick to me like ticks, now, kits! On we go!"

It was clear to him that the rescue party would need to avoid the flooded passageways and cut a fresh side-tunnel into the nursery chamber.

He mustered his most commanding voice and cried out: "Stay together to stay alive, the Really Mads!" The mob motto blazed for the kits in the darkness like a trumpet call. It stirred their blood and lifted their tails and spirits.

Uncle was right to move sharpish. The temperature in the stormy Upworld had dropped close to freezing. The babies would never survive that kind of cold, simple as that. He and the kits set to work with a will to cut a fresh tunnel, but it was painfully hard going. Much of the air had been driven out of the burrow by the gushing water and soon they were all gasping for breath.

"Heave!" urged Uncle. It was touch and

go, but – with just moments to spare – they made it! They broke through the side of the nursery chamber just as the first fingers of water reached in through the main door. In a trice the rising water got them in its icy grip, squeezing out of everyone what little breath they had.

Some meerkats would have turned tail and saved themselves, but not Uncle Fearless. His orders came fast and clear. "Mind out, my dear!" he called to Radiant. "I must pull down the ceiling and get up into Number Five Escape Tunnel, if I can. Kits, stand back and do as your queen says!" With that he began to tunnel as he had never tunnelled before.

"Tally-ho! Stiffen the sinews and all

that!" answered Radiant pluckily, though she was full of dread. "Kits! Help me with the wrigglers. I can only manage Zora."

With Uncle scrabbling furiously, sand and stones splashed down like an avalanche. Skeema, Mimi and Little Dream clamped their teeth into the scruffs of the mewing babies' necks. It was all they could do to keep their tiny heads above the rising tide.

There was no shaft of light to show that Uncle had broken through to Number Five Escape Tunnel, but suddenly there was a welcome blast of life-giving air and a shout of triumph.

"Phew! Relief! No sign of water here! Up you come, my darlings!" called Fearless as he reached down to grab Radiant and little

Zora in his powerful jaws.

Having hauled his wife and one daughter to safety, he turned to the task of pulling up the older kits, each with a littl'un in their teeth. "Move along now, keep moving, quick, quick!" he urged each sodden kit as he lifted them out of the swirling water. "The whole burrow could cave in at any moment!"

Exhausted and shuddering, the Really Mads and their precious bundles staggered along Number Five Escape Tunnel as fast as they could. They moved steadily, up and up the slope towards the entrance to one of the many emergency boltholes.

"We're n-not going to the Upworld before s-suntime, are we?" asked Little Dream nervously, his teeth chattering. He wasn't

26

just thinking of the terrible cold out there. He was worried about all the unseen enemies waiting to pounce in the darkness.

"Don't worry, laddie!" called Uncle. He knew they must stay underground until the sun came out of its hiding place to warm them. His aim was to find a safe, dry hollow or chamber just under the surface where the mob could shelter from the wet. If they could only manage that, they could share the last of their body heat with the almost lifeless newborns.

They struggled on for what seemed an age. Suddenly, a shrill voice stopped them dead.

"Halt! Who goes there?"

Fearless grunted with relief. As challenges go, it was a nervous one and straight away he was sure that it came from a male ground-squirrel. Meerkats and ground-squirrels often share living quarters, but this one had never had visitors. He thought of this remote end of Far Burrow as his own private property. No wonder he was quaking with fright.

"Stand easy!" barked Uncle, gasping for breath. "No danger. Fearless here. King. Really Mads. Bit of an emergency. Flooded out. Babies. Got a soaking. Cold. Can you help?"

"Did someone say babies? Meerkat babies? In danger?" came an anxious female voice. "Of course we can help! *Eeeep!* Emergency drill, squirrels! Gather! Gather to Mother!"

And before the tired-out Nearly Mads could say *Warm-up*, they found themselves

wrapped in the middle of a gloriously welcome hot and furry bundle…

…of neighbours.

Chapter 2

The welcome group-hug put life and warmth back into the Really Mads. And once the ground-squirrels were sure that their visitors were fit to move on, they led them among tangled roots and rocky soil to an empty dugout where there was no sign of any flooding. It smelled as if it might once have been a shelter for a porcupine. There, lying among crunchy bits of beetle-shell, melon skins, tubers and the chewed bones of something far from fresh, at last they managed to get a little well-earned sleep.

It was hunger that eventually woke everyone and set the babies mewing for milk.

"Yikes!" squealed Radiant as the hungriest of the babies started his breakfast. "I say, steady on, Trouble, dear! Your teeth are jolly sharp."

"Ha ha!" chuckled Fearless proudly. "That's my boy! We chose just the right name for him, didn't we, my darling? I always said that one would be Trouble, eh, what! Nice to see a hearty appetite! Just like his bold papa's. I was just the same when I was a little squirmer, wasn't I, my Trubbly-Wubble – tickle-tickle!"

"Hey, I'm starving too!" said Skeema, feeling rather left out.

"Me too!" added Little Dream.

"And me, me! Don't forget Mimi!" wailed their sister. As if anyone could.

Uncle roused himself. "I'd better take a peep outside, Radiant, my fluff," he said, stretching. "You rest here while the kits and I check that the coast is clear. We'll find you something wriggly to keep you going. Then once we've all had a good breakfast," Uncle went on, with a sad note in his voice, "I think we shall have to start looking for a new home."

"Oh, no!" cried Little Dream. "Do we *have* to leave dear old Far Burrow?"

"I'm afraid so. I know how much it means

to you kits, and it breaks my heart to have to leave. Still, I'm afraid it's just not safe any more – especially for the littl'ies. A lot of the escape tunnels will have collapsed already, I'm certain. And what's the most important thing for a meerkat home?"

"If danger's about, you need to get out!" chorused the kits.

"Which means…?" prompted Uncle Fearless.

"Boltholes, boltholes and more boltholes!"

"Right answer!" declared Uncle. "Always be ready for anything! That's the ticket, my clever kits! We're all right for a short while in this rather Whiffy Old Scrape, but it won't do in the long run, what-what! Now, are we all set for a look-about?"

"Not half! I could eat a hippopotamus," declared Skeema.

"Then Upworld, here we come, by all that does and dares!" cried Uncle, and upwards they scurried.

It took only a few moments before they saw the first glimmer of light at the entrance to the tunnel they were in and their hearts began to beat faster. "Steady as we go," said Uncle. Little Dream waited for orders, but Skeema and Mimi were not so patient. They pushed and shoved in a race to be the first to squeeze out of the bolthole and into the sunshine.

"Wait!" said Uncle firmly.

Cautiously, he lifted his nose and sniffed, picking out traces of all manner of creatures:

kudu, zebra, wildebeest, springbok, antelope,
giraffe and elephant. "Hmm, the Big Ones are
gathering in numbers," he muttered. "They're
after the new shoots. No matter. By the smell
of it, I'd say they passed this way a while ago
in the darktime, but you never know."

"Any sign of lions or leopards?" whispered Skeema. "Any cheetahs?"

"Good thinking, my boy!" said Uncle. "Where the great herds go, the pouncers follow, eh? Quiet, now!"

He twitched his sensitive ears in another direction. He heard parrot squawks and bird calls, the clap of storks' bills, the chattering of monkeys in the branches overhead. A low, rasping laugh – "*Herrr-harrr-ha-hah-harrrr!*" – made him duck for cover. "Brown hyenas, by all that's bullying!" he said. The kits clung to him until they felt the tension go out of him. Only then did they start to breathe again. Uncle shook himself free and – ever so cautiously – lifted his head once more and looked about him.

It isn't easy to look around with just one eye. Fearless had to swivel his neck like an owl. *An owl.* Inwardly, he cursed The Silent Enemy, the eagle owl, that long ago had caught him off-guard and swept him up into the sky. Before Fearless had been able to struggle from its grip, the bird had half blinded him. Now, far off, Fearless spied a bateleur eagle circling. Another deadly foe! He muttered a low *Wup! Wup!* but then added softly for the benefit of the others, "As you were. It's a long way away. Good. Stand by to surface."

"Have the rains gone?" came impatient Mimi's voice. "Oh, let Mimi come up and see, me, me!"

"Just keep your fur on while I run through my check list!" barked Uncle. "Now then. Sun's up? Check! Skies blue and clear? Check. No danger up? Check. No enemies close, no runners, no creepers, no sidewinders or crawlers? Check. But dear-oh-dear!"

"What's the matter?" called Skeema.

"You'd better come up and see for yourselves," said Uncle with another sigh.

One by one Skeema, Mimi and Little Dream pulled themselves out of the bolthole entrance, lined up beside him and looked about. They found themselves among the roots of a clump of fever trees that rose from a high patch of rocky ground. Without a word, Skeema took sentry duty at the top of one of them. Horrified, the kits saw at once that streams were running fast into the main entrances to the burrow. A muddy lake had formed in the shallow valley where the yellow foraging-grounds once stretched out. The scrubby bushes and low thorn trees that they knew so well had disappeared under deep water that stretched as far as Shepherd Tree Clump.

"Gone," muttered Uncle. "Far Burrow and all our best hunting-grounds!"

"Take cover!" Skeema called suddenly and Uncle and Mimi and Little Dream threw themselves flat on the damp and still chilly sand. The cloudless blue sky had turned pink

and now began to gabble and honk.

"What's happening, Uncle?" squeaked Little Dream. "Is it an attack?"

"Nothing of the sort," snorted Uncle. "Just a bunch of flamingos, that's all. Quite a sight, eh? They're heading for The Great Salt Pan to feed. They won't harm us. Come along now, let's get on with Warm-up."

Uncle stood tall, placed his paws under his (rather fat) belly and heaved his warming-pad up towards the rising sun. "One-two-three… HUP!" he cried, as he did first thing every suntime. Skeema, Mimi and Little

Dream copied him, pretending that their own

tummies were as big and round as Uncle's

and echoed his "One-two-three... HUP!" as,

grinning round at each other, they hoisted

them high. Sharing a joke always helps when things get tough.

They stood quietly like that, watching the thousands of rosy flamingos flapping busily onward above them, stretching their long necks towards their feeding-grounds.

"I wish I could fly," said Little Dream, pretty much to himself. "Last night I dreamed about flying. Wouldn't it be wonderful to be able to lift yourself up and up… higher than the highest tree in the Upworld?"

"And what would you do then?" asked Uncle affectionately. In the early morning sunlight, he felt some of his customary vim and vigour swelling in him, like the sweet juice that plumps up a wild tomato.

"I would look for Mama," said Little Dream

softly. "And when I found her, I would fly down and lead her home."

Uncle was so touched, he had to clear his throat. "Hurrumph! Lead her *home*, you say?"

He didn't really see how his sister, Fragrant, the kits' mother, could possibly be alive. The night she had gone missing, there had been wild dogs on the loose. No one could seriously believe that a lone meerkat could survive a pack of hungry *Painted Ones* on the prowl. However, he felt sure that this was not the time to say so. The Really Mad Mob had come very close to losing everything dear to them, so his duty as king at the moment was, as he saw it, to keep everyone's spirits up.

"In that case," he added gently, "we shall

just have to make sure we build a splendid new one, shan't we? Meanwhile, we all know what we must do at this present moment, which is…?"

"Get some food inside us and Crack On!" came the resounding reply.

Crack On is the Meerkat Way.

Chapter 3

And even as the meerkat breakfast-party cracked on, some miles away, a two-legged creature had decided that soon he would crack on, too.

A boy, we would call him. And let's call him Shadow because his apricot skin blended with the colours of the shady grove of trees in the centre of which he stooped, gathering up his things.

For some weeks he had wandered alone across the vast, scorching centre of the Kalahari Desert.

It was a test of how strong he was in body and in spirit. Like all the boys of his tribe, he had to go by himself and face sandstorms and hunger and thirst and treacherous paths and mirages. He had been stalked by wildcats and mobbed by packs of dancing jackals. He had leaped over lunging snakes and felt the sting of porcupine quills.

So far, he had come through every test bravely and confidently. And without a map or a companion or any sort of help, he had found his way to an ancient oasis. The Really Mads called the place Green Island.

On his walkabout, Shadow had witnessed some strange and wonderful things and in his head he was already turning them into stories to tell round the fire when he returned home to his family. His favourites were about the bravery of three little meerkat kits. They were so small that they could have stood altogether in the palms of his hands. Yet by working together, they had saved a lion cub who was helpless, lost and starving. And when the cub was captured by hunters, they had set him free.

That was the story he most wanted to tell.

"Soon," he told himself. "I must go home soon."

Chapter 4

Radiant thoroughly enjoyed the snacks they brought back to the Whiffy Old Scrape for her and they all sat together, happily munching in the sunshine.

"If you haven't sucked the juice out of a frill-necked lizard, you haven't lived!" said Skeema with a satisfied sigh as he smacked his lips.

Uncle would have agreed, only he had

just bitten the head off a barking gecko and he thought it would set a bad example if he talked with his mouth full.

"A feast, for me, for Mimi!" cried his niece. Her sharp claws had swept aside a mound of damp sand to reveal a clutch of wiggling white larvae. She gobbled them up like sweets.

"Oh, do hurry up, Mimi!" squeaked Little Dream, who was on top of a drie doring bush taking his turn as look-out. "It's way past time for you to take over from me!" He took off his sunglasses and rubbed his tired eyes, but only for a moment. Unlike most meerkats, he had been born without the dark eye-patches that protect the sky-watcher from the dazzling rays of the desert sun. Many a suntime ago,

he had dug a Safari-man action-doll out of the sand near the pointy mounds where the Blah-blahs camped – far away in the kingdom of the Sharpeyes. He simply could not have managed without Safari-man's cool-looking eye-wear. And Uncle felt the same about Safari-man's stylish pith helmet and safari scarf: he never went anywhere without them.

"Skeema!" said Uncle. "You're pretty good at the scorpion dance these days! Show the babies how it's done."

"Skeema dance, Skeema dance," chirped the babies, clambering over each other to get a front-row seat.

Skeema gave a very nice demonstration of sniffing, listening, turning stones, rapidly

moving the sand and... turning up... a
scorpion!

"Nice work, Skeema. Now, babies, watch
how he dances him. That's it, Skeema, dart
and dodge. Quick and tricky or he'll sting
your nose!

Forward-forward – JUMP!

In-in – and – BACK!

You see, Zora? Watch Skeema, Quickpaws.

Up comes the sting and WHOOPS! – mind-yer-nose! And

Up comes the sting and WHOOPS! – missed-again! And

Up comes the sting and BITE-it-right-off!

Hooray! Well danced, Skeema! Now give Bundle a taste of what you caught. Nice, Bundle? Yum-yum-scrummy, eh? Just wait your turn, Trouble. Trouble! Don't throw sand on Bundle. TROUBLE! Now look. You've buried him! You've made him cough. That's not nice, is it? No, and it's not funny!"

There was the sound of uncontrollable laughter overhead, followed by a *thud* and a squeal from Little Dream.

"Here's a riddle for you, Skeema," said Mimi. "What goes *Ha-Ha-Plop-Ouch?*"

"Easy," said Skeema. "A sentry with the giggles, falling off his perch."

"I'll get you for that!" yelled Little Dream and chased him round the trunk of the shepherd tree. Mimi sensibly decided that now was a good moment for the changing of the guard and whizzed up out of harm's way to take Skeema's place.

"Come along, babies," cooed Radiant, ignoring the kits. "Mummy find you a lizard to lick and then off we all go and have a nice nap in the shade."

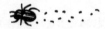

The Really Mad meerkats stretched out in the shadow of the drie doring bush, their bellies nicely full. Radiant lay with her eyes closed, nibbling at a grasshopper. "What a smashing breakfast," she murmured. "Absolutely super. Only…"

"Only what, my beauty?" asked Uncle. "You know I can refuse you nothing."

"Your Majesty is too kind!" laughed Radiant. "It's just that I'm a *tiny* bit concerned that we haven't got enough—"

"Termite larvae?" suggested Skeema.

"Giant millipedes?" put in Little Dream.

"Millipedes, millipedes!" chimed Trouble, and the other babies joined in the chorus.

"No, no! I've had plenty to eat, thank you all," said Radiant. "It's just that, well, apart from the fact that we don't have a proper burrow to call our own, there's something

55

else we're short of. The fact is, there just aren't enough Really Mads to keep us all safe."

"But, my dear…!" spluttered Uncle. "I honestly think I've done a jolly good job of—"

"Hear me out, please," interrupted Radiant. "Just think how much easier things would be in an emergency if there were, well… one or two more of us. I mean, doesn't it worry you that maybe we haven't got enough fighters?"

She paused to attend to one of the babies who was upsetting the others. "No, Trouble, there's a good bubba! Trouble, that's not nice! Ugh! Spit that out, dear! I said… Oh, thank you, lovie. But next time, don't spit things out on to the other babies. Now,

Fearless, as I was saying. There were only just enough of us big and biggish ones to rescue the babies from the flood at Far Burrow. So how is our little mob ever going to protect them if a whopping big meerkat army tries to take over *New Burrow* for themselves?"

"Schemes!" muttered Skeema. He laid his finger across his nose to show that he was talking about something hush-hush. "Plans. I'm good at them. Plus I've got Snap-snap."

"And they would have to get past *me*!" said

SQUEAK!

Mimi, with a flick and a kick and a flash of her feathery headband. "I'm a princess and I don't take prisoners. *Hi-yah!*"

"Jolly nice to know you both have a trick or two up your sleeves," said Radiant. "And your uncle is wonderfully brave. But what if we're hugely outnumbered by invaders?"

"Excuse me," whispered Little Dream, tugging on Uncle's tummy-fur. "Is forty meerkat invaders a hugely outnumber?"

"Well, it's *quite* a hugely outnumber. I mean a huge *number*," said Uncle. "It's, um, let me see, now… is it two against one?" He nibbled his bottom lip as he tried to work it out. "Wait! It's possibly six against one. Why do you ask?"

"Only because I just counted eighty

meerkat eyes peeping over the edge of the sand dune behind us," explained Little Dream. "And half of eighty is forty. That makes forty meerkats. "

"WHA-A-AT?"

"Oh, no, here they come!" yelled Skeema.

Chapter 5

The army of tough-looking meerkat invaders came charging towards the Really Mads at speed.

They threatened and screeched. "Scram and deliver!" they yelled. "Move over for the Massive Mob! Yer burrow or yer life!"

"*WUP-WUP!*" trumpeted Uncle. "ACTION STATIONS! Stand firm, the Really Mads! Battle formation! In line, double-quick, now!

Puff out your fur! Big as you can! Tails, *Hup!* Now quiver 'em! That's it! Now for the old war-dance and battle-chant. Showy as you like! Loud as you can! Altogether, now – one-and-two-and…"

With that, he and his brave little band of warriors let rip.

"*BOUNCY, BOUNCY! BOOM-BOOM, CALL!*

STAND UP, TAIL UP! MAKE YERSELF TALL!

HEAD-BUTT, HEAD-BUTT! STRIKE LIKE A SNAKE!

SPIT-SPIT-SPIT-SPIT! SHAKY-SHAKE-SHAKE!

YOU THINK YOU'RE BIG! YOU THINK YOU'RE BAD!

BUT YOU CAN'T SCARE A REALLY
MAD!"

Oh, the Really Mads did put up a jolly
good show! Even the babies bounced up
and down and blew bubbles. But the enemy
charged nearer and nearer, looking and
sounding more bloodthirsty with every leap
and bound.

"No chance! No chance!" the invaders chanted as they galloped towards the Really Mads. And then they all began to jeer.

"MASSIVE TEETH! MASSIVE CLAWS! MUCH MORE BIGGER-ER THAN YOURS!

HERE'S YOUR WARNIN' IN ADVANCE – YOU AIN'T GOT A FLIPPIN' CHANCE!"

"So horribly rude and rough!" cried Radiant. "How in the Upworld are we ever going to stop these ruffians, Fearless?"

"Stand by to charge!" came his fearless reply.

The Massive Mob hurled themselves onward, closer and closer…

And then – in the blink of an eye-wiper… the enemy ran away.

PHEW!

Uncle was terribly pleased and proud.

"Ah, the old war-dance!" he cried, panting triumphantly. "It's not just a question of numbers, you see, Radiant, my darling. It's all in the old Boom-boom – you follow? It's all in the way you shake it!"

He gave a little demonstration of bottom-waggling. "There!" he boasted. "*That's* what puts the wind up the enemy! The rest of you haven't quite got it, but jolly good show all the same. The main thing was, we all stood together, eh, what?"

A low, growling noise could be heard in the distance, and it seemed to be getting louder and closer at an alarming rate.

"Er… is that a Vroom-vroom, Uncle, by any chance?" Skeema asked timidly.

"What!" cried Uncle. "Is there? Ah! Ah, yes, a Vroom-vroom. Of course, I noticed that! Not that it had anything to do with our victory, naturally! Still, just to be on the safe side… and for the sake of the babies, you understand… *VRRRIPPP! VRRRIPPP!*"

He sounded the retreat and the Really Mads took cover in Whiffy Old Scrape, while he made up his mind what to do next.

Chapter 6

The Vroom-vroom in question stopped not much more than a cheetah's leap from Whiffy Old Scrape.

Uncle sent Skeema to peep out of a well-hidden bolthole to let everyone know what was going on. "Two young eyes are better than one old one," he pointed out. "Now, how many Blah-blahs can you see?"

"Two. Could be one male, one female. But

Blah-blahs all look pretty much the same to me. "

"They're not lion hunters, are they?" asked Little Dream nervously, remembering the brutes that had sneaked up on them that time on Green Island.

"I don't think so. I can't see any nets," said Skeema. "But they've brought a big, round red thing with them. It's lying down on the sand next to its nest. The nest is huge and sort of square."

"A red thing? Lying down? You mean, like a scarlet ibis having a snooze?" suggested Mimi.

"No, it's miles bigger," said Skeema. "Sort of like an elephant, only flat. And red."

"Hmm, a big, round red thing with a square nest! Dashed peculiar," mused Uncle. "We shall have to investigate. Come along." He scrambled out of the hole to look for himself, the kits following close behind.

"Well, if it isn't my old admirer and subject, the Chief of the Click-click tribe!" he exclaimed as soon as he clapped his eye on the Blah-blah. "And he's got a new mate, by the look of it. She's quite a size, eh? Look how long and tottery her legs are! My guess is she may be part-giraffe. But don't be alarmed! She'll soon be paying her respects to me, you'll see. And then you shall all climb *right* to the top of her. Oh, her head will make an excellent look-out post, what-what!"

"Is it safe for the babies to meet them, dear?" came Radiant's anxious voice, for they were all getting restless, especially Trouble. He had just spat on his sister again – twice.

"I don't see why not," answered Fearless. "Why don't we all go over and say how-

d'you-do? They'll be delighted to meet us again, you mark my words!"

The Chief of the Click-clicks – alias Professor Clutterbuck, the great expert on meerkats – along with his mate – also known as Miss Daniela Pipistrella, the world-famous hot-air balloonist and camera-woman – were here to film the next episode of the popular television series, *Kalahari Capers*. Thanks to the radio collar he had fitted on Uncle Fearless some time before, the professor had been able to track Uncle's movements and was anxious to know how he and his little mob of meerkats had managed after the unusually heavy rains.

The professor knew that the rains would

quickly turn everything green on the high plains surrounding the salt pans. That meant that thousands of birds and animals would be crowding there to feed. So he was keen to film the region from the air now that it was teeming with colourful wildlife of all kinds.

At this moment, the pair were concentrating on inflating the balloon and getting Daniela airborne. While the canopy was laid out on the ground, and with the basket turned on its side, Daniela was busy checking the equipment: the liquid-gas cylinders, the burner and the big fan that would eventually direct the hot air from the burner in a stream that would fill the canopy, lifting the balloon and its contents high into the sky above the beautiful Kalahari Desert.

The Blah-blahs' behaviour was strange and not a little worrying to Uncle and the kits. But they stood their ground bravely at what seemed a safe distance and bobbed up and down so that the Blah-blahs would notice them. "Hello! I say! Look this way! We're over here!" called Uncle. But it was no good. They didn't even glance in his direction. "Aha! I think I see what's happening!" he muttered. "They're putting up some kind of shelter! It's probably one of their pointy mounds. The silly things are nesting! Over here, I say!"

"Uncle," asked Skeema mischievously. "Are you sure that the Blah-blahs know how important you are?"

"Of course they bally-well do!" roared Uncle. "How exasperating! We'll just have to go right up and—"

He was interrupted by a shout from the female Blah-blah, followed by a deafening noise like a whole pride of lions roaring at once.

Naturally, it sent all the meerkats scurrying for cover once more.

Chapter 7

"All systems go!" shouted Miss Pipistrella, as the noisy burner flamed and the fan whirred. Lying on its side in the sand, the canopy of the one-man balloon began to swell with hot air. "Is the tether-rope securely tied to the towbar of the pickup? The balloon will start to lift up any moment now."

"Yes. It's lashed on tight. You say the word and I'll stop the fan."

"That'll do," shouted Daniela with a wave, and the fan stopped. "She's rising. Give us a hand!" she yelled and the professor ran to help. With a one two-three-*heave*, they got the basket upright and the great bubble of the canopy billowed above it. The balloon rose about a metre above the truck until it was caught by its tether rope and could climb no higher. Daniela scrambled up on to the bonnet of the pickup, leaned into the basket and threw a switch. Instantly, the burner died.

For a minute there was a shocking silence and then hundreds of birds and insects, as though they'd been holding their breath, filled the silence with their rasping and creaking and twittering.

"How long will she hover without more hot air?" asked the professor.

"Oh, quite a while," replied Daniela. She looked up at the steel frame that held the burner. "Could you pass me my bag? It's got my camcorder and some water and stuff in it."

No sooner had he done so then Daniela

staggered and had to throw out her arms to regain her balance. The balloon suddenly lurched sideways and its tether-rope jolted the truck.

"Whoa!" yelled the professor. "I say! The wind's getting up!"

"You're right," agreed Daniela. "It's too risky to fly right now." She hopped out of the basket. "I'll wait until it's calmer." Suddenly, a movement on the ground a little way off caught her eye. "Gosh! Look over there!" she exclaimed.

"Well, I never…" laughed the professor.

At last the Really Mads had the Click-clicks' full attention!

Uncle was issuing instructions to his

little mob. "Right! One more time! Bunch together, Really Mads!" he cried. "When I say the word… give 'em another waggle!"

Emerging from behind a tuft of dry elephant grass, the Really Mad Mob waggled their bottoms with all their might.

The Click-clicks were enchanted. Cautiously, they moved towards the waggle-bottoms, dropped to their knees and raised their eye-protectors in front of their faces. *Click-click*, they went.

"About time too!" crowed Uncle, pulling himself up to his full height. "Some proper respect at last, what-what! This way, now, babies. Don't be afraid. They won't hurt you. They just want to pay their respects to Papa."

Bundle, Zora and Quickpaws were fascinated by the strange antics of these large creatures. In no time they plucked up the courage to try some of the broken bits of boiled egg that were held out for them to nibble.

As for Trouble, he soon got bored. He was far more interested in the big red thing floating above the Vroom-vroom.

He slipped away without anyone noticing, and in two shakes of a rock-python's tail, he had hopped on board the basket.

Chapter 8

"Trouble, where are you? You come back here!" shouted Mimi. She and her brothers had been sent on an urgent rescue mission with orders to find the runaway and return him to his mama and papa immediately. The kits clambered, panting, over the sides of the big, square nest woven out of wickerwork. There was no sign of him at all.

Suddenly, they heard a rustle coming from

inside what you or I would recognise as a large handbag. "Come out of there at once!" Skeema ordered. "Your mama and papa are very worried about you!"

"Mind The Silent Enemy doesn't swoop down and peck your eye out," added Little Dream. "Like what happened to your papa when he was young and all by himself with no one keeping a look-out for him!"

"Peck eye out," came a sad muffled voice from inside the bag.

"We meerkats have to stick together to stay alive," Skeema reminded him.

"Stay alive," came the muffled voice, but still he didn't come out.

Mimi reached in and grabbed him by the scruff of his neck.

"Yikes!" She got rather a shock. Trouble had stumbled on some make-up in the Blah-blah's bag and had smothered himself in bright colours. There was black on his cheeks and a black line between his eyes, red and brown all over his body.

"Ha ha!" laughed Skeema. "He looks like a little wild dog! What a fine disguise!"

"Find da skies!" echoed Trouble.

"What else have we got in here?" asked Skeema. He burrowed into the bag at once. It was rather a squash because Little Dream had decided to have a look at the same time.

"This reminds me of the time I sneaked a look round an empty jackal's lair," giggled Little Dream, rummaging away. "They steal things from Blah-blahs, you know. They go for shiny stuff like this." And indeed the Blah-blah's bag was full of bits and pieces that shone and sparkled, a treasure trove of things they had never seen before…

"Hey! What about this?" he added. "This is the shiniest thing."

"Baggsie me have that!" cried Skeema and popped out to look at it properly in the light. Little Dream didn't mind. To him, the sprays and the lipstick were strange beetles in hard, bright shells. They looked delicious.

As for Skeema, he was delighted with his

chain that had a flat polished stone hanging from it. He held the stone up to his eye and found that he could see right through it!

Trouble squealed with fright.

"What's up with him, Mimi?" Skeema asked, seeing the baby clinging to her for dear life.

"Your eye!" she told him. "It's grown as big as a kudu's!"

"Really?" said Skeema, putting down the little magnifying glass. "My eye feels quite normal to me."

"Well, it is, now that you've stopped looking through that pebble," said Mimi.

"How odd!" said Skeema, and looked at Little Dream through it. "Oo-er, Dreamie!" he said. "You've turned into a big baboon!"

"Give it to me! I want it!" cried Mimi, trying to put the chain round her neck. "I've been wishing and wishing for something nice to wear to go with the quills and feathers on my headband."

"No way!" declared Skeema, snatching it back, and putting the chain round *his* neck instead. "Why should you get all the interesting things?"

"Because I'm a princess! I need special things!" came the angry answer.

"What about this?" suggested Little

Dream, popping out of the bag with his latest find. "I don't know what it is, but it's nice and soft." This was his first sighting of a pair of leopard-print knickers.

It was Mimi's too, and she cheered up at once. "Perfect! It's for carrying babies!" she declared. "Hop in the baby-carrier, Trouble, and I'll take you home in it. Pop those squirty things in too," she added, taking the spray bottles from him and putting them, and Trouble, in her new baby-carrier.

Little Dream was chewing away at one

of his finds. "Disgusting!" he spluttered and spat it out.

"I say! What's happened to your lips, Dreamie?" asked Skeema. They had gone bright red.

"Just as I thought. There *was* a millipede hiding in this hard shell," said Little Dream, holding it up, "but it tastes horrible! But look at this! Hurray! A Blah-blah eye-protector!" he shouted, casting the millipede to one side. And he put the strap of the little camcorder round his neck.

Suddenly, a violent gust of wind caught the balloon. The tether-rope that anchored it to the bumper-bars of the pickup truck was stretched tight and everyone was thrown about.

Trouble gave a squeal as Mimi staggered. He tried to cling to the side of the nest. Instead, he pulled down a switch and

SHHHHRAAAAAAAAAAAAAAAAAH!

A great tongue of flame came roaring out of the burner and swelled the drooping canopy overhead. In an instant, it was puffed up like a giant ostrich egg.

"Everybody out! Run for your lives!" yelled Skeema and dived over the side.

But it was too late for the others. With a rip and a *twang* and a tearing of metal, the tether-rope snapped the bar it was tied to, and the balloon shot into the air.

Chapter 9

Rocketing through the blue like furry astronauts, Mimi, Little Dream and baby Trouble thought the end had come.

For a while, they lay bundled up together in the bottom of the basket, scared to death by the terrible noise and the leaping fire above their heads. "I'm going up too fast!" wailed Mimi. "I'm going to hit the sun!"

It was Little Dream who gathered his thoughts together first. "What did you touch?" he yelled into the pouch on his sister's back. "Can you show me, Trouble?"

Trouble's head appeared, his bright eyes blinking nervously.

"Show you," he said quietly, pointing his nose in the direction of something shiny sticking out of one of the nest's walls.

"You mean this?" yelled Little Dream, and gave it a poke upwards. Immediately the horrible noise stopped and the flame went away.

For a moment, there was a wonderful hush. And then there came a faint cry from just below them. "*Helk! Helk!*"

"That sounds like Skeema!" said Mimi. "And he's in trouble! Where is he?"

Three corners of the basket were taken up by liquid-gas cylinders, but there was a hole in the other one, so Mimi and Little Dream were able to put their heads out and look down. The shock of what they saw took their breath away.

Below them, Uncle Fearless and Radiant and the three babies they were holding were not much bigger than dung-beetles. The truck and the horrified-looking professor and Miss Daniela Pipistrella were shrinking fast. They rapidly went from baboon-size to meerkat-size to lizard-size to beetle-size to ant-size. The wrinkly mounds in front of Whiffy Old Scrape were fast becoming –

well – just wrinkles.

The cliff that towered above the burrow became a long, shadowy line and the grassy plain came into view, stretching away to the mountains.

"Wow," said Mimi. "This is scary! What's that whopping great grey-blue cloud down there? Termites?"

"Gildegeeste," came Skeema's voice again. "A huge big crowd of them nunning together!"

"Where are you, Skeema? And why are you talking funny?" called Mimi.

"Here I ang! Down here!" came Skeema's voice, sounding more and more agitated.

SKWEEEEE! came Snap-snap's war-cry.

It was then that Mimi caught sight of

her brother hanging on for dear life to the
tether-rope, with Snap-snap squeezed between
his teeth.

"Can you climb up?" asked Little Dream. "You'll be safer in here with us. Do try!" And so Skeema struggled up the tether-rope, up the wickerwork sides of the basket – and it wasn't long before Little Dream and Mimi had their teeth in the furry scruff of Skeema's neck and were hauling him back into the nest.

"Thanks!" puffed Skeema, putting Snap-snap down safely on the floor. "Phew! What's going on, exactly?"

He couldn't help noticing that Little Dream had a blissful smile on his face. "Look here, Dreamie!" he said indignantly. "We're all in a very tight spot! What are you smiling about?"

"We're flying!" said Dreamie. "This is

what I dreamed about. Isn't it lovely?"

"Nubbly," echoed Trouble.

"Is *that* what I'm doing?" asked Mimi. "I say! It is rather fun!" She climbed up the side of the basket so that she and Trouble could get a better view. "So that moving lake down there, the one made out of black and white stripes. That must be..."

"Zebra," said Skeema. "Hundreds of them. It's just like Uncle always says," he continued in hushed tones. "You can't tell where one of them stops and the next one starts. Brilliant, eh? It must be very confusing for lions, don't you think? They must find it jolly hard to know where to pounce!"

It didn't take long before he began to enjoy himself too. "I see what you mean about this flying business, Dreamie," he said. "It's a bit like swimming, really, isn't it? Only not so wet, of course. I didn't think it would be this quiet, though. Listen."

They strained their ears and they could make out the rumble of hooves, a distant mooing, a whinny, a faint yap – that sort of thing, but all very far away.

"It is lovely, Dreamie," said Skeema quietly, "but how are we going to get down?"

"Oh, dear," Little Dream muttered. "We're all alone, and we haven't got a single bolthole to run to. If only Uncle were here to tell us what to do!"

Chapter 10

At the moment when the wind jerked the kits and their precious naughty baby high into the air, Radiant and Fearless felt completely helpless.

"Surely there's *something* we can do, Fearless, my love!" Radiant said at last as the balloon began to shrink into the distant sky. "We can't just let them go like that!"

Fearless was in shock. All at once

he found himself reliving the terrifying moment when he was caught off-guard by The Silent Enemy and had been swept up into the air himself. He felt the shocking rush of that vertical take-off in his belly. His paw went up to his empty eye-socket as if to protect his eye from a cruel hooked beak. He remembered the struggle to get his claws and teeth into the enemy and how he had fallen then, tumbling over and over in the air until the ground came up with a sickening crash. The pain was suddenly as bad as if it had just happened.

It was all he could do to stop himself from trembling. But then he gave himself a shake-up that sent electric sparks crackling through his puffed-out coat of fur. He was Fearless again.

"Stand by! No time to waste!" he declared. "We must go after them immediately!"

"Right away, my love! We mustn't lose heart," said Radiant. "Whatever it takes, we'll find them!"

"Whatever it takes!" said Uncle, managing a smile.

"And no matter how far!" said Radiant, blinking away a tear.

"Then we shall have to go like the wind, what-what!" declared Uncle.

Suddenly, the Blah-blahs leaped into their Vroom-vroom and made it roar. Radiant and the babies flinched.

"By all that jars and makes you jump!" exclaimed Fearless. "Those Blah-blahs must be going after their nest! And if anything can run like the wind, it's one of those Vroom-vrooms! Come on! We must get on it somehow!"

Already, the pickup had begun to move, but away they went after it, fur flying, ready to risk everything to keep the Really Mads together.

"Professor! Did you see what I just saw?" exclaimed Daniela Pipistrella, tightening her seatbelt as the pickup began to gather speed. "In the rear-view mirror, I mean?"

"If you mean, did I see a bunch of meerkats hopping into the back, then I certainly did!" he replied with a chuckle. He glanced in the mirror again, but could see little more than a billowing cloud of sand thrown up behind.

"Those little meerkats never cease to amaze me," he went on. "See if you can get a few snaps of them, will you? Now, if we're going to catch up with that blessed cloud-hopper of yours before nightfall, I shall have to put my foot down. Hang on!"

Vrooom – vrroooom!

Chapter 11

And *hang on* is just what Skeema, Mimi, Little Dream and Trouble were doing, as their balloon flew across the endless sands of the Kalahari.

"Why can't we hear the wind?" asked Little Dream.

"I think it must be because we're riding on it," said Skeema.

There was a whirring sound. Some bright

parrots flapped past, squawking and arguing. Next came a flock of elegant egrets and some dazzlingly white avocets; then a crowd of purple glossy starlings, chip-chipping away.

"All right, mate? All right, mate?"

"All right, mate!" chirped Trouble, popping up and showing his painted face. He got one or two rather old-fashioned looks before the nervous birds tipped their wings and darted off across the blue.

"This nest we're in," said Mimi. "It was

roaring before. How come it's stopped roaring?"

"And spitting fire!" said Skeema enthusiastically. "What's happened to the fire?"

"The fire just sort of popped down into its burrow when I flipped this thing," said Little Dream, indicating the switch.

"I wish I knew how to make fire! Then I could scatter all our enemies and Radiant wouldn't need to worry about the Really Mads needing more fighters."

"Why don't you wish for something more useful – like us being able to get down from here," demanded Mimi.

"Why don't you just be quiet for once?" replied Skeema angrily.

Little Dream was ignoring them both and playing with his new eye-protector. "I had one of these once that went flash," he muttered half to himself. He tried pressing a button on the top and was pleasantly surprised. It began to whirr, a bit like grasshoppers do before you bite their heads off. And he found he could see through a window at the back into a little world that was exactly like the world below, only much smaller. It was very soothing.

He was shocked out of his trance by some very excited and rather angry squawking and flapping.

"Oo-er," he said, as he lifted the eye-protector and found that its window was full of strange-looking pink birds.

"Eek! I'm in the middle of a flock of flamingos!" cried Mimi.

"Bingos!" repeated Trouble, rather fascinated.

None of the meerkats had ever been this close to a crowd of flamingos before, and they came as a bit of a shock. There was something about the way their necks stretched out in front and their long, skinny legs trailed out behind them that Skeema didn't like. As for the horrid flat, webbed feet floating along on the ends of those legs, they looked as if they could give you a nasty slap! And worse than their big feet were their giant, hooked beaks and their mad round eyes...

"How're you doing, ladies?" asked Skeema with a gulp, hoping that a bit of charm might stall them if they were about to attack.

"Hoy! Do you mind?" said one of the

birds flapping right alongside the basket. "I may be pink, but I am a big tough bloke, so you watch it."

"You wochit!" echoed Trouble.

"Right, sonny," said the nearest flamingo, dipping one black-tipped wing to bring himself even closer to the basket. "You are going to get a beak up the bracket for that!"

Trouble decided not to wait around to find out where his bracket was. He popped out of his baby-carrier like a cork out of a bottle and grabbed the red cord that hung down from above. There was a ripping sound as the top of the canopy opened up. Hot air rushed out through the hole and the balloon dropped like a stone.

Chapter 12

"*EEEEEEEEEEK!*" squealed Skeema, Mimi and Little Dream, feeling that their tummy-pads had been sucked out through the hole in the canopy with the hot air.

Trouble made a similar sound as he swung on the red cord and sicked up his breakfast at the same time.

"See if you can get the fire to roar again, Little Dream!" cried Skeema. "That might make us go up instead of down."

Little Dream strained to move the switch. "No good," he grunted. "It won't budge."

"Trouble! Get back in your carrier NOW!" ordered Mimi in her bossiest voice. Amazingly, that did the trick and Trouble did as he was told. He let go of the red cord and dropped back into his carrier with a *plop*.

Straight away the hole in the top of the canopy closed and the balloon stopped falling and levelled out. The trouble was, now that it was closer to the ground, things seemed to be rushing at it even faster than before. The kits peered out and found that they could recognise where they were. A curving gash of rippling blue cut through the desert below. "Look. That must be

Wild River!" gasped Skeema, as things began
to make sense to him.

Little Dream began to recognise things
too. "Those round silver things leading off

into the distance like shimmering stepping stones must be the salt pans! We ran across them once, before the rains came. Do you remember?" said Little Dream excitedly.

"When I had that dream about following Mama's footsteps and we found some footsteps to follow, only they weren't Mama's, they were made by—"

"Griff!" interrupted Mimi. "Down there, by those shady trees, look! I'm sure it's him!" She called to him as loudly as she could and the others joined in: "*Griff! GRIFF!*"

And sure enough, stretched out in the cooling shade, lay a lion cub protected by three lionesses. It just had to be their sweet-tempered lion-cub friend, now safely reunited with his mama and two aunts – The Three Graces.

"I don't think they've seen us. They must be asleep," said Skeema.

"Then wave! *Make* them look!" insisted Mimi because they were flying past them fast.

And since the others couldn't see the point of waving, Mimi decided to do it herself. She shrugged the baby-carrier off her back. "Hold the baby!" she ordered and thrust him into Skeema's arms. Trouble rescued the two little bottles of spray from the bottom of the bag, holding one tightly in each front paw, before Mimi whisked the bag away. Then she was up and leaning over the side of the basket.

As anyone who has ever waved a pair of leopard-print knickers will know, they are just the job for attracting attention. But sad to say, Griff and the lionesses, having eaten well, were far too sleepy to notice anything much, and the balloon passed overhead without them ever knowing.

But at least one pair of sharp eyes turned in wonder and astonishment to gaze at the sky. Shadow had just left Green Island. He had clambered over the low rocks scattered at the edge of it. He had begun to jog purposefully homeward across open country, when something made him duck back and crouch out of sight behind a low boulder. He had seen many wonderful sights on his walkabout. Yet he never expected to see anything quite as breathtaking as this.

He saw a basket, held up by some sort of rippling, giant red bubble, drifting silently across the sky on the stiff breeze – and rapidly losing height! There was something in the basket, moving restlessly. Was it the head of a leopard? No, it was a piece of cloth that was marked with spots like a leopard. But what was holding it? Not a meerkat, surely? It was! And look! There was another meerkat peeping over the top of the basket... and another...

Ayeee! Shadow was at once delighted and shocked. He knew those faces! How strange. How wonderful. And how alarming. Where were all these brave little creatures flying to?

He lifted his gaze then and saw, riding on the wind just above the flying puffball, an escort of graceful flamingos. Then he noticed with alarm something else circling silently, even higher! It was a bird of prey, an eagle owl, its great wings spread.

It was The Silent Enemy!

"At last!" The Silent Enemy said to himself. "The waiting is almost over. Fearless, their uncle, has escaped me twice now. Twice he has made me suffer. Those fat little meerkats are in my power. They will serve nicely as my supper and my sweet revenge!"

Chapter 13

Mimi was still waving at the lions when Little Dream picked out Green Island over to his right. He remembered Green Island well. It was the place where the pawprints had led him and his brother and sister, denting the powdery crust of the dry salt pans. He had hoped that the prints would lead to where his lost mama would be waiting. Instead, the kits found Griff the lion cub, lost and starving and in need of their help.

"It's no good," said Mimi with a sigh. "Nobody can see me."

The wind had shifted slightly and the basket was tilting now. Green Island was shrinking away and the cloud-hopper was dropping lower and lower, gliding fast in the direction of another island… a pink one!

A *pink* one?

"I didn't know they had pink islands," said Little Dream. "You don't suppose it's going to come up and crash into us, do you?"

Before any of the kits (or even Trouble, who wasn't really of an age to think about anything much) could answer, there was a loud commotion in the sky ahead of them. Curving round in a wide rosy arc from somewhere high above and behind them, hundreds of flamingos were lining up, two-three-four-abreast, so that they could head into the wind for landing. Their destination was not an island at all, but a lake formed by the recent rains that filled The Great Salt Pan.

"*Honk!*" cried the first wave of them as they realised that they were on a collision course with a big red flying elephant. "*Honk-honk!* Mind out, you great lump! Give over! Shove out the way! Can't you see you're in our flight-path?"

"Brace yourselves!" ordered Skeema, taking charge. "Some of them might hit us!"

Mimi put her arm behind her, grabbed Trouble and pulled him tight to her, and Little Dream curled up like a porcupine. As for Skeema, who had the heart of a lion, he had the presence of mind to pop Snap-snap into his mouth to sound a challenge and a warning – *SKWEE! SKWEE! SKWEE!*

"Use the eye-protector, Dreamie!" he called. "See if you can get it to flash and scare the blighters off!"

Up jumped Little Dream, boldly facing the rushing mass of swirling pink. There was no flash, sadly, only a weak little *Whirr* noise, not loud enough to out-shout a mosquito. Still, he stood firm, shoulder to shoulder with

Skeema, certain that any moment the first wave of birds with their enormous, hooked black beaks would crash into them, punch the stuffing out of the canopy and send the kits in the basket plunging down to splatter like rare raindrops on the desert sand.

The balloon was now flying low enough for everyone to be able to smell a dreadful stink. Skeema turned his gaze downward and was astonished to see *thousands* of flamingos standing together on their stilt-like legs, their heads upside down in the water and sweeping from side to side. The lake smelt so bad it made his eyes water. *And that*, thought Skeema, *is where we are all going to end up – in that filthy mess – drowned!*

Chapter 14

Luckily, a stiff wind is a fickle thing. One minute it'll be heading for The Great Salt Pan, teeming with the newborn shrimp and algae that give the millions of flamingos their fabulous colour as they feed. Next minute it'll change its mind and breeze off in quite another direction.

"Phew!" said Skeema. "That was a close one."

But they were far from out of danger as it was only now, when he saw that they were at their most helpless, that The Silent Enemy decided to make his move.

He folded his wings and dropped out of the sun like fizz-fire. He gave no cry; he made no sound. Surprise and silence were his best weapons.

As he dived closer to the basket, he leaned back, stretching out his feet and opening his wings a little, so as to slow himself down. He wanted to make sure he aimed his talons bang on target.

"Oo-hooo!" he gloated to himself. "I'm longing to see the fright in their eyes!" He knew that they would freeze with fear, like all the other kills he had made. They would

give up and let themselves be snatched away. *Look at them clinging together!* he thought. *I shall take all three at once!*

It was true; they did see him (all except Trouble, who had taken cover in his baby-carrier) as they clung to each other in terror. They saw his terrible eyes, they saw his terrible pointed ears, heard his screech of triumph. They couldn't take their eyes off the sharp curves of the claws that reached for them. It flashed across Skeema's mind that The Silent Enemy's powerful chest had an almost- perfect pattern of spots and bars on it. The only thing that spoilt it was an untidy cluster of feathers that refused to be preened into place. Right on his breastbone there was an untidy battle-scar. That was where Uncle Fearless had sunk his teeth.

And that was exactly where Shadow's arrow struck home with a *thwack*!

Little Dream was sharp enough to hear the *twang* of Shadow's bow. His eyes widened as he caught a glimpse of a two-legged creature standing close to a spreading acacia tree, still holding the bow in his outstretched arm.

Next thing, a tangle of brown and white was spinning towards the ground.

Bubo Africanus, The Silent Enemy, was dead.

"The Silent Enemy!" cried Little Dream. "That creature saved us from him!"

"What creature?" cried Mimi and Skeema, looking over the edge of the basket where

Little Dream was looking. But the boy was nowhere to be seen.

As the kits turned back from the edge of the basket, they realised they had no time to celebrate. They were hardly more than a giraffe's neck from the rock-scattered ground beneath, and they were rushing towards six great, red ebony trees that stood like giants watching over the vast desert sands.

"Red Ebony Point ahoy!" called Captain Skeema. "Hang on to me and brace yourselves, chaps!"

"Look out!" screamed Mimi, as first they bounced and skidded over the top of a low acacia tree. The rattle of the twigs across the bottom of the wicker basket was terrifying. Then came an

ear-splitting racket from a colony of
weaver birds who felt the tremor
run through their dangling
nests, thatched apartments
that hung just
underneath the
shady top.

Still the balloon raced on – but disaster lay just ahead. "Help!" screamed all of the kits at once. There was no avoiding the enormously tall, red ebony tree right in front of them. With a deafening crash, the canopy was slashed to shreds by tearing branches and instantly, the basket swung on its ropes and was smashed against the trunk.

In a few seconds, two of the gas cylinders had burst, and the basket was awash with liquid propane, the whole thing exploding in a massive ball of fire.

Shadow was close enough to feel the heat of the explosion when it came. He flung himself flat on his face and in that way avoided being shot through with bits of twig and branch that flew like arrows at him.

When he looked up, he had to raise his arm to shield himself from the awful heat. The upper branches of the ebony were crackling with flames. Soon the whole tree was blazing like a torch and sending up a plume of smoke thick enough for any creature within thirty miles to see.

Of his brave little meerkat friends, there was not a sign.

The pickup was less than a mile away at the time of the explosion. By driving like a madman, Professor Clutterbuck had almost caught up with the runaway cloud-hopper. He and Daniela Pipistrella had been watching its progress anxiously for the last five minutes, only too aware that it was losing height fast.

They could hardly bear to watch as they saw the balloon head straight for an enormous, red ebony tree.

"Oh, no! Please, no!" wailed Daniela and clutched the professor's arm.

As the fireball blossomed in the sky just over the ridge, the professor swung the driving-wheel, jammed his foot on the brake and brought the pickup to a grinding halt. The cloud of dust that had been following the pickup caught up with it and everything disappeared in the choking cloud.

That included Fearless, Radiant and the babies. As soon as the professor hit the brakes, they'd been shot into the air… right over the cabin of the pickup. Luckily, they had a soft landing in the middle of a tsamma-melon bush.

When the dust cleared, they looked about anxiously, not even taking time to dust themselves down. More than anything else, they hoped to see that the flying Blah-blah

nest had landed softly on the ground. But to their bitter disappointment and misery, what they actually saw was a gigantic tree on fire and the last shreds of red material being eaten up by hungry flames among its top branches. As for the nest carrying the kits and their precious baby – it had vanished like smoke.

Chapter 15

In fact, the meerkat kits had been catapulted out of the basket of the burning balloon – first on to the lower branches of the ebony, then into a driedoring bush, and then on to the desert sand.

For a while they lay silent, stunned and still in the burning sun. Then they picked themselves up, as they knew they must, and ran together to get under the sheltering branches of the acacia tree that they had so nearly crashed into.

When a colony of weaver birds is upset, they let everybody know it. They get into a flap. "This is bad. This is a bad time! No more visitors!" they cried, dozens of them whistling past the ears of Skeema, Mimi, Little Dream and baby Trouble. "First we have snakes moving in among the egg-sitters in the darktime! Swallowing our eggs! Snatching our fledglings! Then along comes a big noise, then this fire, this smoke! And who invited them? Not us! Not us! *Chirroo! Chirroo!* So we don't want you! *Shoo!*"

Never mind that these visitors were badly battered and fearfully frit, and all they needed was a place to recover from their fall and shelter from the coming dark and all the enemies it hid… The meerkat kits got buzzed, they got bombed and they got threatened. *Chirrrrooo! Keep out! Scram!*

That's weaver birds for you. But weaver birds don't worry meerkats. Noisy as it was under the spreading branches of the acacia tree, they were safe here for the moment.

"Everyone OK?" panted Skeema.

"OK," said Trouble, peeking out nervously from behind Mimi. The others were stunned into silence for a moment, but meerkats can't afford to waste time feeling sorry for themselves. They checked to see if any bones were broken. No. Bruises didn't count.

In a daze, the kits looked about them for cover. They were quick to see a hollow

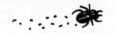

among the roots at the base of the tree.

"Why don't we get in there?" suggested Little Dream, still trembling.

"Not yet," said Skeema. "There might be something living down there already. There could be a rock-monitor or anything. I suggest we just lie low here until we get our strength back."

He knew that to be out in the open with no bolthole to run to is not the meerkat way. The Silent Enemy might be dead, but that still left plenty of room for a martial eagle or a goshawk. And apart from the branches above them, there was precious little beyond in the way of bushes or thick grasses or other ground cover – only some remarkably tall ebony trees, one of them black now and still smoking. Thankfully, the other trees were not standing close enough for the fire to be able to jump on them. Not that that was much comfort. Not to a small mob of little meerkats far from home. Their heads were full of cheetahs that might come sprinting at them, and swarming packs of jackals or hyenas.

Then Trouble began to mew with hunger. Having sicked up his breakfast, he was starving.

"Want Mama! Hungry!" he cried sadly.

"Where are we? What are we going to do?" said Little Dream quietly.

"Hush, everyone!" whispered Skeema. "You never know who's listening!"

And indeed somebody was listening, and watching them too. It was Shadow.

Shadow was kneeling by a thorn bush not far away. He had recovered his arrow from the body of the eagle owl he had shot down and was now intent on tying the creature's legs together with twine made from woven grasses.

He had almost finished this task when the cries from Trouble made him jerk his head to see where they came from. The bright white of his eyes and teeth lit up his shining face. So his little friends had not been blown to pieces when their flying-machine had exploded! And there was a baby with them. A painted baby!

Some time ago, in Green Island, he had entered the cave sacred to his ancestors and painted a picture of himself on the wall. He had also drawn these meerkats because they were special to him. And now, very gently, he spoke three words of friendship to them in his language, the language of the San people. The words he spoke were, "Go, safe, home."

Of course, meerkats cannot speak the language of any Blah-blah, from any tribe. But the San language is full of gentle clicks, and the Really Mads had no fear of a gentle click or two. They stood quite still and watched the boy as he reached into his leather bag and drew out a handful of nuts, berries and still-wiggling grubs. He placed some in his own mouth and chewed eagerly to show they were safe. Then he laid the rest in a small heap in front of him on some fallen leaves.

Having offered this gift, his next moves were smooth and silent. He pulled a feather from the limp body of the eagle owl and blew it into the air as a sign that he wished the little meerkats luck next time they went flying. Then he slung his kill over his shoulder. He was planning to roast The Silent Enemy for his supper. He picked up his spear and his bow, stood upright and took a deep breath.

He had a long way to go. He had worked out that before he arrived home, he might need to light three campfires for himself – perhaps four. But then he would be back among his people. He would share the family-fire, the family-feast, and then he would sing the story of the magic meerkats. He would sing of the little warriors who could tame lions and who knew how to fly.

He would dance them being blown to pieces and he would dance them back to life again!

He was ready. He had no more business here. In three clicks he was off and running.

"Go. Safe. Home."

It was Little Dream who ran over and picked up the feather. His keen nose caught not just the scent of The Silent Enemy. There was another scent that he had smelled in the cave on Green Island.

"Do you remember the shapes we saw on the wall?" he asked his brother and sister. "We saw shapes in the cave on Green Island that looked like meerkats. And there was another shape that looked like a young Blah-blah. That was him! Don't you see? We found him – or he found us!" He got no reply, so he added, "He was the one that saved us from The Silent Enemy!"

But the others weren't listening. Their minds were concentrated on the food spread out on the table of dry leaves. They sniffed the offerings and found them good.

"Go ahead," said Mimi. "Try one of these, Trouble. They're lovely."

"Ubbly," said Trouble, and tried three.

"Come on, Dreamie, come and eat!" said Mimi with her mouth full.

"Shhhh!" ordered Skeema. He sat up, ears cocked, nostrils twitching. "I can smell something! There! The wind's blowing it from that direction." He was pointing to a rise beyond the scattering of drie doring bushes.

Trouble let out a squeal as Mimi grabbed him between her teeth and ran like the wind to take cover under the bushes. The others dashed alongside, hissing "Quiet! Quiet, Trouble! You'll give us away."

When they were safely out of sight and the baby was hushed, Skeema sneaked to the top of the ridge to spy out on the land.

It only took him a moment for his eyes to confirm what his nose told him. He dashed back to the hiding place with the news.

"What is it?" whispered Mimi.

"A male meerkat," whispered Skeema. "A *huge* one! He's got a burrow over there and he's spraying scent-marks all round the entrance. Strong ones. A lot of them."

"He must be a king," Little Dream said, trying to explain to Trouble. "It's a warning. It means *Keep away, strangers! Or else!*"

"Keep away!" repeated Trouble, who had heard that one before.

"We could keep away," pondered Skeema. "But if we do, he might send out his big army to attack us anyway. I think we should go to that king and introduce ourselves and ask for protection. Maybe he'll take us in."

"Yes, and maybe his army will beat us up!" snorted Mimi.

Skeema could see that the others weren't convinced. "All we have to do is explain that we haven't got a burrow of our own," he pleaded. "And we'll say that we don't have a mama or a papa to look after us."

He knew it sounded feeble. Worse than that, it set Trouble off. "Mama! Papa!" he wailed, bursting into tears.

A sudden *yap-yip-yap-yip* silenced them all as terror swept over the kits. They had good reason to be scared. That ghostly, high-pitched gabble and the scuffle of galloping feet in the sand were close! They were sounds they all dreaded. There it was again. *Yap-yip!*

It was the hunting-call of *The Painted Ones*.

"Wild dogs!" whispered Little Dream with a shudder. More cunning even than jackals or hyenas, wild dogs are cleverer hunters and stronger fighters. Sometimes known as painted dogs because of their bright colours, a pack of them spreads terror wherever they go. There is no fiercer nor more dangerous an enemy in the Upworld.

Chapter 16

Little Dream's shuddering outburst made Mimi and Skeema shake and shiver too. Though they tried to look calm for the sake of the baby and to say nothing, they each had the same thought: *Like the ones that killed Mama.*

Wishing that Uncle Fearless was there to give them all courage, Skeema made a big effort to get his worried mind to work properly. He gripped Snap-snap tight and tried to stand as tall as he could. *A safe place. Where? Not here!*

"Shake yourselves up, Really Mads!" he cried, hoping that he sounded confident. At once there was a rattle and *snap*, like flags streaming out in the wind, as everybody put some sparks into their fur and made themselves big.

"Those brutes are hungry. We'll have to make a dash for the hollow under the weaver-bird tree."

"But you said there might be a rock-monitor down there!" yelled Mimi. "Those things are worse than crocodiles!"

"That's a risk we'll have to take," urged Skeema. "Because sure as scratch-yourself there are *definitely* wild dogs on the rampage. And they're coming this way. Let's go!"

Mimi grabbed Trouble in her jaws, having lost her baby-carrier in the explosion, and raced after the others to the hole that Skeema hoped would save them.

He had just started to plunge into it, when there was a roar from the darkness.

"Halt!" ordered the rumbling voice.

"Ahh! It's the rock-monitor!" screamed Mimi.

"Wait! Listen!" said Skeema. The voice came again, not at all hissy and hungry, but strong and brave. "Who goes there?" it demanded.

"PAPA!" shrilled Trouble's excited voice from just behind Skeema.

"Uncle!" cried the older kits. "But how…?"

"By all that's weird and wonderful!" exclaimed Uncle with delight. "There! I told you they'd make it, my fluff! But goodness, you did give us a shock when we saw that nest explode!"

"My little lost loves!" came Radiant's voice, equally thrilled to see them all again.

"Trouble! Trouble! It's Trouble!" squealed Bundle, Zora and Quickpaws in delight.

And what a moment it was. What a squeaking, squealing SQUEEZE there was in that dark, tight place. What relief! What tears of joy!

"Oh, my goodness!" cried Radiant when she saw little Trouble for the first time.

"What have you got all over your face? You
looked quite scary for a moment, my little
baby!"

Uncle chuckled. "That's my boy! A true
warrior! Now, steady on, the RMs!" Uncle
barked.

"How in the Upworld did you get here?" exclaimed Mimi.

"Well now, that's quite a story, by all that zigs and zags, but it will have to wait till later," said Uncle urgently. "The main thing is that right now, we've taken shelter in this hollow in order to get away from a starving pack of *The Painted Ones*! I imagine that's exactly what you're doing too. A marvellous piece of luck for us all, what-what! But listen. We may all have escaped those hellhounds for a short while, but we must save our joy and our delight for later. This place is not safe." The cuddling and the nuzzling stopped at once. "Radiant and I realised that when we darted in here. And mark my words – if those painted pouncers don't find something to eat soon, they'll smell us and dig us out like termites!"

"Spot on, as usual, my lovie!" exclaimed Radiant. "There's no back door to this hole. We're no safer here than ants in an aardvark's pantry."

Fearless had never spoken more urgently. "Think now, kits. Did you have a chance to do a bit of scouting? Is there *anywhere* near here we could make a run for?"

Mimi piped up in the dark. "The only other shelter round here is a meerkat burrow. I found it earlier over a rise not far away. The only thing is, it's occupied by strangers."

"What do you mean *you* found it?" cried Skeema indignantly.

"Never mind who found it," said Radiant.

"Tell us – are the occupants friendly, do you happen to know?"

"Army!" squeaked Trouble. He remembered the bit about the army.

"I see," said Uncle. "A big army, I suppose?"

"Actually, we only saw the king," said Little Dream. "But he's *very* big and strong."

"Then I think we should throw ourselves on his mercy, for the sake of the kits and the babies," said Radiant, making up her mind.

Uncle wasn't so sure. "I take your point, my beauty. But do we really want to go bowing and scraping to strangers? I'm a king, let me remind you!"

"And I'm your queen," said Radiant. "But what other choice have we got? We must think of the little ones."

She was right and Uncle knew it. "You're quite right, my sweetness!" he cried. "We must make a dash for the strangers' burrow for the sake of the squirmers."

He was squeezing past them all as he spoke and in a second his keen nose was thrust out into the bright and dangerous desert air. The hot stink of wild dog hung there still, but fainter than before. Fearless turned to speak quietly to Skeema. "Is there any cover at all between here and the burrow entrance? I wouldn't put it past those dogs to be lying in wait."

"Thorn bushes," answered Skeema. "About halfway between here and there."

"That's something, I suppose," said Fearless. "Up you come then, everyone.

Now keep together, RMs! *Wup! Wup! Wup!*
Charge for the bushes!"

And away they went like furry fizz-fire.

Chapter 17

A wild dog can run at forty miles an hour for a short while, and it can keep running at thirty miles an hour for a lot longer. He also knows when to lie still and wait. That is just what the hungry pack of *The Painted Ones* were doing. They had spread out and were waiting patiently to ambush anything that moved past. As soon as they saw the meerkats make a dash for it, they were on their trail like lightning.

"In here! This way!" called Skeema, and the Really Mads dived for cover into the prickly heart of the thickest bush. Bundle, Zora and Quickfire had done their own running, but Mimi had got used to minding Trouble and had carried him in her mouth.

A high-pitched *yap-yip* silenced them. It was close. Very close! A wild dog was sniffing around the edge of the bush, looking for a painless way in.

Trouble didn't like the smell of the wild dogs. Before anyone could stop him, he wriggled out from the safety of the bush. He popped out right in front of the *Painted One* who was scratching away at the thick outer twigs and branches of the bush.

"YAP-YIP!" yelled Trouble.

The dog was so shocked that he pronked like a springbok. When he hit the ground again, he found himself face to face with a tiny painted terror! In the Kalahari, anything brightly painted is likely to be deadly. Up went the dog's crazy round ears. "*Arrrgggh!*" He let out a scream and backed off, whining.

At that moment, another dog turned up. "What are you doing, you mug!" he growled. "You scared of a little squirt like that? Get 'im!"

Squirt was exactly the right word. Trouble stood his ground. Still holding his squirty bottles, one in each hand, he pressed down on both buttons at once.

FSSSSS! FSSSSS!

"*Ayeeeeeee!*" howled the dogs and rushed off with their tails between their legs.

"Good shooting, my boy!" cried Uncle, grabbing hold of Trouble and hauling him back to safety. "Right in their eyes like an oogpister beetle! You're as tricky as your cousin Skeema!"

But there was not much time to celebrate.

More painted dogs arrived, angrier and hungrier than ever, all sniffing around the bush, looking for a way in.

"I've got an idea! It may not work," said Skeema grimly, tugging at the shiny pebble on the chain round his neck. "But it's our only chance. Let's see if I can scare them off with the Big-Eye trick."

"Go for it, Skeema!" cried Mimi.

The sun, now lower in the sky, was behind Skeema as he sneaked out from the bush. As he turned, the sun seemed to catch on the stone round his neck, shooting out a little shining point of light. It landed on a tall tuft of dry weed. He could hear the dogs all around, scratching with their greedy paws.

Skeema thought at first that the light

might be some sort of bright beetle or butterfly with sparkling wings. But then he noticed that when he moved the shiny stone, the bright light moved too. And when he held it still for a moment, a little twist of smoke rose from the grass.

Suddenly, the breeze picked up. At once it carried Skeema's smell to the eager nostrils of the wild dogs. They let out whistling cries of triumph and delight.

"Wassat?"

"Get 'im!"

"Tear him to pieces!"

But the same breeze puffed the smoke in the dry grass into a little flame. "Fire!" Skeema whispered to himself in delight.

"Everyone! Get behind me! NOW!"

he shouted, and the Really Mads obeyed, watching the scene unfold in wonder.

First there was a crackle. Then a rush of fire. "*Ayeeeeeee!*" And then the whole tuft went up in flames. A nearby tuft caught alight then – and then another. Away went the dogs, howling and yelping. In a flash, they were heading towards the setting sun.

"Bye bye, doggies!" said Trouble and his words were picked up by the other babies.

"*Bye-bye! Bye-bye!*" chanted Zora, Bundle and Quickpaws.

Uncle looked around proudly at the Really Mads, standing strong together again. It brought a tear to his eye. "Mustn't let meself down by blubbing, now!" he murmured. He watched with the others as the pack of

dogs disappeared into the distance, the fur scorched off their retreating backsides.

Wild dogs are famously fast runners, as we know. But as Skeema put it with a chuckle, "When there's a fire behind them, I bet they can go faster than cheetahs!"

As luck would have it, the flames didn't spread and they died down almost as quickly as they had sprung up. Then the babies got over-excited and rolled in the ashes, covering themselves in black.

"You silly, silly things!" said Radiant and Uncle cheerfully, happy to get busy by licking the little blighters clean.

"That was very silly, Skeema," Mimi scolded. "Fire can jump and spread!"

"You're right," said Skeema. Something in him was delighted. After all, his wish to be able to make fire had come true. But the heat of the flames had singed his eyebrows and taught him a hard lesson. He ran the back of a wet paw over the sore places to sooth them. "Don't worry. I shan't do it again," he promised, his heart pounding.

"Good work!" came a powerful voice from the top of the dune. "I never thought we'd see the back of those thugs!"

Chapter 18

The powerful figure who called out to the Really Mads was none other than the meerkat male that Skeema had seen spraying his scent so furiously around the entrance to his burrow.

"Welcome, brave meerkats. My name is Broad Shoulders of the No Name tribe. Perhaps you would be so kind as to introduce yourselves and tell me your business here."

"My name is Fearless," said Uncle. He was polite, but wary. Meerkats are never comfortable with strangers or with the unknown. For them, it is a terrible thing to be in unfamiliar territory. "This is my queen, Radiant. These are our babies. These kits are my sister's children." He puffed out his proud chest. "We call ourselves the Really Mads."

"Are there no more of you?" asked Broad Shoulders, scanning them all carefully.

Uncle was uneasy. He remembered the talk of an army. He decided not to answer the question and instead asked one himself. "The darktime is coming. Do you know of a safe place for us to shelter?"

Broad Shoulders was at a loss for a moment. "Well… the dogs have gone," he said. "They won't risk coming back here in a hurry."

"It's for the little ones," explained Radiant.

"Will you forgive me?" said the stranger, looking uneasy himself. "It's my wife. My queen, you understand. I need to see how she feels. She hasn't heard the news about the wild dogs yet. She can't bear them, you see. As a matter of fact, she's so terrified of them that she wouldn't even leave the burrow to feed. So you see…" His words trailed off.

"There's no shame in fear," said Radiant. "Wild dogs are as bad as The Silent Enemy. Worse, in a way, because they hunt in packs. It takes a team effort to outwit them."

Little Dream smiled to himself. He was still clutching the feather from the dead body of The Silent Enemy. Now was not the time, but he would give it to his Uncle later.

"A team effort. Ah, yes. Exactly so," said Broad Shoulders. "But the fact is, my wife was once chased by wild dogs when there was not a soul to help her. She was completely alone at the time, and—" He stopped and shook himself. "I'm sorry. I must speak to her in her chamber. Would you mind just waiting here for a moment? I shan't keep you long." And with that he hurried into the burrow.

"I don't like this, my dear," said Radiant in a low voice. "There's something fishy going on here. What kind of a name for a mob is the No Names? And what if he's gone to call out his fighters? Who knows if we shall have the strength to fight an army after all that's happened? I think we should leave while we can."

"Now? When it will be cold and dark soon?" asked Uncle gently. "Are you sure, my love? The babies have had enough to put up with since the floods came to Far Burrow, don't you think?"

"Very well," said Radiant. And so they waited.

"Shoulder to shoulder now," said Uncle.

"Sharp and tricky! Be prepared for anything!"

As it turned out, though, that was a hard order to follow. For when at last the queen of the No Names came out of the dark burrow, escorted only by her husband, King Broad Shoulders, no one was prepared for such a lovely sight. Her smooth and elegant coat of fur seemed to blaze in the late-afternoon sunlight. Her gentle face and shy, smiling mouth was touched with worry and pain, yet it was perfectly shaped and delicate. Her searching gaze swept across the faces of the silent Really Mads. Then quite unexpectedly, she gasped, clutched her heart and uttered a little sobbing cry.

Be prepared for anything! Uncle had said. But no one had been expecting this. No one

except for Little Dream, who had hoped
against hope. It was he who broke the silence.

"Mama!" he whispered. "I knew we'd find
you."

Chapter 19

A few meters from the No Name Burrow, next to the overheated pickup truck, Professor Clutterbuck and Miss Daniela Pipistrella were putting up a tent. They had been surprised to see patches of burned grass on the way to this spot, but guessed that sparks must have somehow carried from the burning tree where the balloon had crashed. They had spent quite a bit of time wandering about by that tree, looking for anything that might have fallen from the balloon.

They didn't say much as they pegged the tent down tight, but they were quietly content, and they hummed a tune together as they worked. Every now and then, they would stop, look at each other, shake their heads, shrug their shoulders – and laugh.

This may seem strange, given that they had seen Daniela's cloud-hopper – that they had needed to film the next episode of *Kalahari Capers* – blown to smithereens. But as it happened, all was not lost. For, having searched around the crash-site, they had been surprised to find two objects, both of which brought smiles to their faces and made them feel a lot better.

One of these objects was frilly and spotted like a leopard. You can probably guess what it was a pair of!

The other was Daniela's camcorder. By some miracle, it was in perfect working order! And when she started playing it back, she let out a shriek of astonishment and delight. There was wonderful footage of the rolling plains, teeming with wild game – everything you could hope to see in a film about the Kalahari: wildebeest, zebra, giraffe, antelopes, lions; you name it! As for the shots of flamingos – they were *unbelievable*! The viewer was actually flying along in the middle of a great flock of them, hearing their calls and the beating of their wings! And then you were looking down on The Great

Salt Pan *crammed* with feeding birds, spread out below like a bowl full of pink rose petals. Fabulous!

Then there was something even more unexpected. "Hey! You're never going to believe *this*!" Daniela had exclaimed, as she and the professor gathered round to watch the screen. And there, to their delight, were the most charming scenes of little meerkats scampering all round the basket, looking over the side, chattering at birds flying by.

The professor, who had spent a lot of time studying these meerkats, recognised them all: they were the three kits he'd filmed many times before, and their new little sibling, who had somehow managed to smear bright colours all over himself.

"They are so *cute!*" said Daniela.

Of course, the professor took his study of meerkats very seriously. He never thought of them as *cute*. But even *he* had to agree that one of the most charming things he had ever seen was the shot of the little female leaning over the side of the balloon waving— well, you know jolly well what she was waving. So let's spare the blushes of Miss Daniela Pipistrella, the world-famous balloonist and camera-woman, and not keep mentioning it.

Later, as they were sitting round the campfire, Daniela said quietly, "I wonder if any of the kits could have possibly survived the crash."

"Well, I'm getting a very strong signal from Fearless's radio collar, so he's definitely

nearby," said the professor. Whether he
or any of the others who jumped into the
pickup, are alive, I..."

"I do hope so," said Daniela with feeling. "They deserve a new start after being flooded out of their old home."

"Well, it's getting dark now," said the professor, "so we shall just have to wait till tomorrow before we can track down the signal and find out exactly what has happened to our brave little meerkats."

As we shall see, they were in for a very nice surprise...

Together at last, Fragrant and her lost kits! How she held them! How they breathed her in and whimpered for joy to be bathed in the scent of her once more. She clasped them as tightly as she had when she first nursed them, long ago. And even when she was certain that they were real and she had told them over and over that she would *never* leave them, not *ever*, she had to keep touching them and nuzzling them to be sure that she was not dreaming.

And then there were stories to be told. How Fragrant was cast out of her burrow by a jealous queen; how she had wished to die and had almost been killed by a pack of painted dogs. How she struggled on, a wanderer, an outcast, until by chance she had met her handsome prince, Broad Shoulders. Like her, he had no tribe, but they swore to be true to each other and to stay together, even if they had no name. Out of *No Name*, they made a new name for themselves, and here, in this remote and

lonely place, they also made a secret home together.

"Why a secret home, Mama?" asked Little Dream.

"Because we were so few," she whispered. "We decided to lie low together until the babies came."

"The babies?" asked Radiant. "You mean…?"

"Yes," said Fragrant shyly. "There will soon be some brothers and sisters for Mimi and Skeema and Little Dream."

"Yippee!" exclaimed Skeema. "More fun for us!"

"We like babies," agreed Little Dream.

"We *love* babies! Even naughty ones," laughed Mimi. "Isn't that right, Trouble?"

"Love trouble!" cried Trouble in delight.

"There, Radiant! You wanted a bigger mob and now you've got one!" cried Uncle. "And with Broad Shoulders to fight with us, I reckon we can put on a good show if it comes to a scrap over territory!"

"We should be honoured to call ourselves Really Mads, sir, if you will join us and make this your home," said Broad Shoulders respectfully.

"What do you say, my queen?" asked Fearless.

"Gosh!" said Radiant with a sigh. "What a suntime! Well, I for one am jolly pleased to take up that offer!"

"And so say all of us!" cried the kits.

"All us," yawned Trouble, cuddling up

to his doting papa, while Radiant cuddled Bundle, Zora and Quickpaws.

"You squeak when you're squoken too, you naughty baby!" laughed Radiant.

"You're not naughty, are you, my lad?" cooed Fearless. "Just *advanced* and full of spirit! I was just the same when I was a kit. By all that nips and tucks, I've got some stories I could tell you…"

"Hush, dear," said Radiant. "We've all got stories to tell about how we got here. But I think we should put the babies to bed now. It's time they settled into their new chamber."

"In their new *home*, what-what!" chuckled Uncle.

Little Dream twiddled the feather of The Silent Enemy. Should he give it to Uncle now? No, let him see it in sunlight. No time for much talking now. "And where shall we kits be sleeping this darktime, Mama?" he asked shyly, wallowing in the warmth of her lovely fur.

"Why, where you all belong, of course," she murmured. "With me. With Mama."

The funniest stories starring the wildest wildlife...

RACCOON RAMPAGE

HANG OUT WITH
THE HOLE-IN-
THE-TREE GANG!

ANDREW COPE

Jeanne Willis

Penguin Pandemonium

The Rescue